Guest Book

Guests

Name and Relationship to Parents

Advice for Parents

Wishes for the Baby

Guests

Name and Relationship to Parents

_____

_____

_____

Advice for Parents

_____

_____

_____

_____

Wishes for the Baby

_____

_____

_____

_____

Guests

Name and Relationship to Parents

_____

_____

_____

Advice for Parents

_____

_____

_____

Wishes for the Baby

_____

_____

_____

Guests

Name and Relationship to Parents

_____

_____

_____

Advice for Parents

_____

_____

_____

Wishes for the Baby

_____

_____

_____

Guests

Name and Relationship to Parents

_____

_____

Advice for Parents

_____

_____

_____

Wishes for the Baby

_____

_____

_____

Guests

Name and Relationship to Parents

_____

_____

_____

Advice for Parents

_____

_____

_____

Wishes for the Baby

_____

_____

_____

Guests

Name and Relationship to Parents

Advice for Parents

Wishes for the Baby

Guests

Name and Relationship to Parents

_____

_____

_____

Advice for Parents

_____

_____

_____

_____

Wishes for the Baby

_____

_____

_____

Guests

Name and Relationship to Parents

Advice for Parents

Wishes for the Baby

Guests

Name and Relationship to Parents

_____

_____

_____

Advice for Parents

_____

_____

_____

Wishes for the Baby

_____

_____

_____

Guests

Name and Relationship to Parents

Advice for Parents

Wishes for the Baby

Guests

Name and Relationship to Parents

_____

_____

_____

Advice for Parents

_____

_____

_____

Wishes for the Baby

_____

_____

_____

Guests

Name and Relationship to Parents

Advice for Parents

Wishes for the Baby

Guests

Name and Relationship to Parents

_____

_____

_____

Advice for Parents

_____

_____

_____

Wishes for the Baby

_____

_____

_____

Guests

Name and Relationship to Parents

Advice for Parents

Wishes for the Baby

Guests

Name and Relationship to Parents

_____

_____

_____

Advice for Parents

_____

_____

_____

Wishes for the Baby

_____

_____

_____

Guests

Name and Relationship to Parents

Advice for Parents

Wishes for the Baby

Guests

Name and Relationship to Parents

_____

_____

_____

Advice for Parents

_____

_____

_____

Wishes for the Baby

_____

_____

_____

Guests

Name and Relationship to Parents

_____

_____

_____

Advice for Parents

_____

_____

_____

Wishes for the Baby

_____

_____

_____

Guests

Name and Relationship to Parents

_____

_____

_____

Advice for Parents

_____

_____

_____

Wishes for the Baby

_____

_____

_____

Guests

Name and Relationship to Parents

Advice for Parents

Wishes for the Baby

Guests

Name and Relationship to Parents

_____

_____

_____

Advice for Parents

_____

_____

_____

Wishes for the Baby

_____

_____

_____

Guests

Name and Relationship to Parents

_____

_____

_____

Advice for Parents

_____

_____

_____

Wishes for the Baby

_____

_____

_____

Guests

Name and Relationship to Parents

_____

_____

_____

Advice for Parents

_____

_____

_____

Wishes for the Baby

_____

_____

_____

Guests

Name and Relationship to Parents

Advice for Parents

Wishes for the Baby

Guests

Name and Relationship to Parents

_____

_____

_____

Advice for Parents

_____

_____

_____

_____

Wishes for the Baby

_____

_____

_____

Guests

Name and Relationship to Parents

_____

_____

_____

Advice for Parents

_____

_____

_____

Wishes for the Baby

_____

_____

_____

Guests

Name and Relationship to Parents

_____

_____

_____

Advice for Parents

_____

_____

_____

_____

Wishes for the Baby

_____

_____

_____

Guests

Name and Relationship to Parents

_____

_____

_____

Advice for Parents

_____

_____

_____

Wishes for the Baby

_____

_____

_____

Guests

Name and Relationship to Parents

_____

_____

_____

Advice for Parents

_____

_____

_____

Wishes for the Baby

_____

_____

_____

Guests

Name and Relationship to Parents

Advice for Parents

Wishes for the Baby

Guests

Name and Relationship to Parents

_____

_____

_____

Advice for Parents

_____

_____

_____

Wishes for the Baby

_____

_____

_____

Guests

Name and Relationship to Parents

Advice for Parents

Wishes for the Baby

Guests

Name and Relationship to Parents

_____

_____

_____

Advice for Parents

_____

_____

_____

Wishes for the Baby

_____

_____

_____

Guests

Name and Relationship to Parents

Advice for Parents

Wishes for the Baby

Guests

Name and Relationship to Parents

_____

_____

_____

Advice for Parents

_____

_____

_____

Wishes for the Baby

_____

_____

_____

Guests

Name and Relationship to Parents

Advice for Parents

Wishes for the Baby

Guests

Name and Relationship to Parents

Advice for Parents

Wishes for the Baby

Guests

Name and Relationship to Parents

Advice for Parents

Wishes for the Baby

Guests

Name and Relationship to Parents

Advice for Parents

Wishes for the Baby

Guests

Name and Relationship to Parents

_____

_____

_____

Advice for Parents

_____

_____

_____

Wishes for the Baby

_____

_____

_____

Guests

Name and Relationship to Parents

_____

_____

_____

Advice for Parents

_____

_____

_____

Wishes for the Baby

_____

_____

_____

Guests

Name and Relationship to Parents

Advice for Parents

Wishes for the Baby

Guests

Name and Relationship to Parents

_____

_____

_____

Advice for Parents

_____

_____

_____

Wishes for the Baby

_____

_____

_____

Guests

Name and Relationship to Parents

Advice for Parents

Wishes for the Baby

Guests

Name and Relationship to Parents

_____

_____

_____

Advice for Parents

_____

_____

_____

Wishes for the Baby

_____

_____

_____

Guests

Name and Relationship to Parents

Advice for Parents

Wishes for the Baby

Guests

Name and Relationship to Parents

_____

_____

_____

Advice for Parents

_____

_____

_____

Wishes for the Baby

_____

_____

_____

Guests

Name and Relationship to Parents

_____

_____

_____

Advice for Parents

_____

_____

_____

Wishes for the Baby

_____

_____

_____

Guests

Name and Relationship to Parents

_____

_____

_____

Advice for Parents

_____

_____

_____

_____

Wishes for the Baby

_____

_____

_____

Guests

Name and Relationship to Parents

_____

_____

Advice for Parents

_____

_____

_____

Wishes for the Baby

_____

_____

_____

Guests

Name and Relationship to Parents

_____

_____

_____

Advice for Parents

_____

_____

_____

_____

Wishes for the Baby

_____

_____

_____

Guests

Name and Relationship to Parents

_____

_____

Advice for Parents

_____

_____

_____

Wishes for the Baby

_____

_____

_____

Guests

Name and Relationship to Parents

_____

_____

_____

Advice for Parents

_____

_____

_____

Wishes for the Baby

_____

_____

_____

Guests

Name and Relationship to Parents

Advice for Parents

Wishes for the Baby

Guests

Name and Relationship to Parents

_____

_____

_____

Advice for Parents

_____

_____

_____

Wishes for the Baby

_____

_____

_____

Guests

Name and Relationship to Parents

Advice for Parents

Wishes for the Baby

Guests

Name and Relationship to Parents

_____

_____

_____

Advice for Parents

_____

_____

_____

Wishes for the Baby

_____

_____

_____

Guests

Name and Relationship to Parents

_____

_____

_____

Advice for Parents

_____

_____

_____

Wishes for the Baby

_____

_____

_____

Guests

Name and Relationship to Parents

_____

_____

_____

Advice for Parents

_____

_____

_____

_____

Wishes for the Baby

_____

_____

_____

Guests

Name and Relationship to Parents

_____

_____

_____

Advice for Parents

_____

_____

_____

Wishes for the Baby

_____

_____

_____

Guests

Name and Relationship to Parents

_____

_____

_____

Advice for Parents

_____

_____

_____

Wishes for the Baby

_____

_____

_____

Guests

Name and Relationship to Parents

_____

_____

_____

Advice for Parents

_____

_____

_____

Wishes for the Baby

_____

_____

_____

Guests

Name and Relationship to Parents

_____

_____

_____

Advice for Parents

_____

_____

_____

_____

Wishes for the Baby

_____

_____

_____

Guests

Name and Relationship to Parents

_____

_____

_____

Advice for Parents

_____

_____

_____

Wishes for the Baby

_____

_____

_____

Guests

Name and Relationship to Parents

_____

_____

_____

Advice for Parents

_____

_____

_____

Wishes for the Baby

_____

_____

_____

Guests

Name and Relationship to Parents

_____

_____

_____

Advice for Parents

_____

_____

_____

Wishes for the Baby

_____

_____

_____

Guests

Name and Relationship to Parents

_____

_____

_____

Advice for Parents

_____

_____

_____

Wishes for the Baby

_____

_____

_____

Guests

Name and Relationship to Parents

Advice for Parents

Wishes for the Baby

Guests

Name and Relationship to Parents

_____

_____

_____

Advice for Parents

_____

_____

_____

Wishes for the Baby

_____

_____

_____

Guests

Name and Relationship to Parents

Advice for Parents

Wishes for the Baby

Guests

Name and Relationship to Parents

_____

_____

_____

Advice for Parents

_____

_____

_____

Wishes for the Baby

_____

_____

_____

Guests

Name and Relationship to Parents

_____

_____

Advice for Parents

_____

_____

_____

Wishes for the Baby

_____

_____

_____

Guests

Name and Relationship to Parents

_____

_____

_____

Advice for Parents

_____

_____

_____

_____

Wishes for the Baby

_____

_____

_____

_____

Guests

Name and Relationship to Parents

_____

_____

_____

Advice for Parents

_____

_____

_____

Wishes for the Baby

_____

_____

_____

Guests

Name and Relationship to Parents

_____

_____

_____

Advice for Parents

_____

_____

_____

_____

Wishes for the Baby

_____

_____

_____

_____

Guests

Name and Relationship to Parents

_____

_____

Advice for Parents

_____

_____

Wishes for the Baby

_____

_____

Guests

Name and Relationship to Parents

_____

_____

_____

Advice for Parents

_____

_____

_____

Wishes for the Baby

_____

_____

_____

Guests

Name and Relationship to Parents

Advice for Parents

Wishes for the Baby

Guests

Name and Relationship to Parents

_____

_____

_____

Advice for Parents

_____

_____

_____

_____

Wishes for the Baby

_____

_____

_____

Guests

Name and Relationship to Parents

_____

_____

_____

Advice for Parents

_____

_____

_____

Wishes for the Baby

_____

_____

_____

Guests

Name and Relationship to Parents

_____

_____

_____

Advice for Parents

_____

_____

_____

Wishes for the Baby

_____

_____

_____

Guests

Name and Relationship to Parents

_____

_____

_____

Advice for Parents

_____

_____

_____

Wishes for the Baby

_____

_____

_____

Guests

Name and Relationship to Parents

_____

_____

_____

Advice for Parents

_____

_____

_____

Wishes for the Baby

_____

_____

_____

Guests

Name and Relationship to Parents

_____

_____

_____

Advice for Parents

_____

_____

_____

Wishes for the Baby

_____

_____

_____

Guests

Name and Relationship to Parents

_____

_____

_____

Advice for Parents

_____

_____

_____

Wishes for the Baby

_____

_____

_____

Guests

Name and Relationship to Parents

_____

_____

_____

Advice for Parents

_____

_____

_____

Wishes for the Baby

_____

_____

_____

Guests

Name and Relationship to Parents

_____

_____

_____

Advice for Parents

_____

_____

_____

Wishes for the Baby

_____

_____

_____

Guests

Name and Relationship to Parents

Advice for Parents

Wishes for the Baby

Guests

Name and Relationship to Parents

_____

_____

_____

Advice for Parents

_____

_____

_____

_____

Wishes for the Baby

_____

_____

_____

_____

Guests

Name and Relationship to Parents

Advice for Parents

Wishes for the Baby

Guests

Name and Relationship to Parents

_____

_____

_____

Advice for Parents

_____

_____

_____

Wishes for the Baby

_____

_____

_____

Guests

Name and Relationship to Parents

Advice for Parents

Wishes for the Baby

Guests

Name and Relationship to Parents

_____

_____

_____

Advice for Parents

_____

_____

_____

Wishes for the Baby

_____

_____

_____

Guests

Name and Relationship to Parents

Advice for Parents

Wishes for the Baby

Guests

Name and Relationship to Parents

_____

_____

_____

Advice for Parents

_____

_____

_____

Wishes for the Baby

_____

_____

_____

Guests

Name and Relationship to Parents

Advice for Parents

Wishes for the Baby

Guests

Name and Relationship to Parents

_____

_____

_____

Advice for Parents

_____

_____

_____

Wishes for the Baby

_____

_____

_____

Guests

Name and Relationship to Parents

Advice for Parents

Wishes for the Baby

Guests

Name and Relationship to Parents

_____

_____

_____

Advice for Parents

_____

_____

_____

_____

Wishes for the Baby

_____

_____

_____

_____

Guests

Name and Relationship to Parents

_____

_____

_____

Advice for Parents

_____

_____

_____

Wishes for the Baby

_____

_____

_____

Guests

Name and Relationship to Parents

_____
_____
_____

Advice for Parents

_____
_____
_____
_____

Wishes for the Baby

_____
_____
_____

Guests

Name and Relationship to Parents

_____

_____

_____

Advice for Parents

_____

_____

_____

Wishes for the Baby

_____

_____

_____

Guests

Name and Relationship to Parents

_____

_____

_____

Advice for Parents

_____

_____

_____

_____

Wishes for the Baby

_____

_____

_____

_____

Guests

Name and Relationship to Parents

_____

_____

_____

Advice for Parents

_____

_____

_____

Wishes for the Baby

_____

_____

_____

Guests

Name and Relationship to Parents

_____

_____

_____

Advice for Parents

_____

_____

_____

_____

Wishes for the Baby

_____

_____

_____

Guests

Name and Relationship to Parents

_____

_____

_____

Advice for Parents

_____

_____

_____

Wishes for the Baby

_____

_____

_____

Guests

Name and Relationship to Parents

_____

_____

_____

Advice for Parents

_____

_____

_____

_____

Wishes for the Baby

_____

_____

_____

Guests

Name and Relationship to Parents

_____

_____

_____

Advice for Parents

_____

_____

_____

Wishes for the Baby

_____

_____

_____

Guests

Name and Relationship to Parents

_____

_____

_____

Advice for Parents

_____

_____

_____

Wishes for the Baby

_____

_____

_____

Guests

Name and Relationship to Parents

Advice for Parents

Wishes for the Baby

Guests

Name and Relationship to Parents

_____

_____

_____

Advice for Parents

_____

_____

_____

Wishes for the Baby

_____

_____

_____

Guests

Name and Relationship to Parents

_____

_____

_____

Advice for Parents

_____

_____

_____

Wishes for the Baby

_____

_____

_____

Guests

Name and Relationship to Parents

_____

_____

_____

Advice for Parents

_____

_____

_____

_____

Wishes for the Baby

_____

_____

_____

_____

Guests

Name and Relationship to Parents

Advice for Parents

Wishes for the Baby

Guests

Name and Relationship to Parents

_____

_____

Advice for Parents

_____

_____

_____

Wishes for the Baby

_____

_____

_____

Guests

Name and Relationship to Parents

Advice for Parents

Wishes for the Baby

Guests

Name and Relationship to Parents

Advice for Parents

Wishes for the Baby

Printed in Great Britain
by Amazon

28821099R00071